In Our Neighborhood

Meet a Sanitation Worker!

by Jodie Shepherd

Illustrations by Lisa Hunt

Children's Press®
An imprint of Scholastic Inc.

Special thanks to our content consultant:

Dan Colleluori, Supervisor of Recycling & Sanitation
City of Stamford
Stamford, CT

Library of Congress Cataloging-in-Publication Data
Names: Shepherd, Jodie, author. | Hunt, Lisa, 1973– illustrator.
Title: In our neighborhood. Meet a sanitation worker!/by Jodie Shepherd; illustrations by Lisa Hunt.
Other titles: Meet a sanitation worker
Description: First edition. | New York: Children's Press, an imprint of Scholastic Inc., 2021. | Series: In our neighborhood | Includes index. | Audience: Ages 5–7. | Audience: Grades K–1. | Summary: "This book introduces the role of sanitation workers in their community"— Provided by publisher.
Identifiers: LCCN 2021058731 (print) | LCCN 2021058732 (ebook) | ISBN 9781338768855 (library binding) | ISBN 9781338768862 (paperback) | ISBN 9781338768879 (ebook)
Subjects: LCSH: Sanitation workers—Juvenile literature. | Refuse and refuse disposal—Juvenile literature.
Classification: LCC HD8039.S257 S537 2021 (print) | LCC HD8039.S257 (ebook) | DDC 628.4/42—dc23
LC record available at https://lccn.loc.gov/2021058731
LC ebook record available at https://lccn.loc.gov/2021058732

Copyright © 2022 by Scholastic Inc.

All rights reserved. Published by Children's Press, an imprint of Scholastic Inc., *Publishers since 1920*. SCHOLASTIC, CHILDREN'S PRESS, IN OUR NEIGHBORHOOD™, and associated logos are trademarks and/or registered trademarks of Scholastic Inc.

The publisher does not have any control over and does not assume any responsibility for author or third-party websites or their content.

No part of this publication may be reproduced, stored in a retrieval system, or transmitted in any form or by any means, electronic, mechanical, photocopying, recording, or otherwise, without written permission of the publisher. For information regarding permission, write to Scholastic Inc., Attention: Permissions Department, 557 Broadway, New York, NY 10012.

10 9 8 7 6 5 4 3 2 1   22 23 24 25 26

Printed in Heshan, China 62
First edition, 2022

Series produced by Spooky Cheetah Press
Prototype design by Maria Bergós/Book & Look
Page design by Kathleen Petelinsek/The Design Lab

Photos ©: 7: Terry Whittaker/2020VISION/Minden Pictures; 9: Jupiterimages/Getty Images; 11: Claudia Gannon/Alamy Images; 12: Jeffrey Isaac Greenberg 13+/Alamy Images; 18: NoDerog/Getty Images; 20 left: Walter Zerla/Getty Images; 21 right: Citizen of the Planet/Education Images/Universal Images/Getty Images; 21 left: Daniel Acker/Bloomberg/Getty Images; 23: Jim West/Science Source; 25: Gary Coronado/Houston Chronicle. Used with permission; 31 bottom right: Kinekoo/Dreamstime.

All other photos © Shutterstock.

Table of Contents

Our Neighborhood.................. 4

Meet Celia...................... 8

Cleaning the Streets.............. 14

The Recycling Center.............. 22

▶ Ask a Sanitation Worker......... 28

▶ Celia's Tips................... 30

▶ A Sanitation Worker's Tools..... 31

▶ Index......................... 32

▶ About the Author............... 32

OUR NEIGHBORHOOD

Hi! I'm Theo. This is my best friend, Emma. Welcome to our neighborhood!

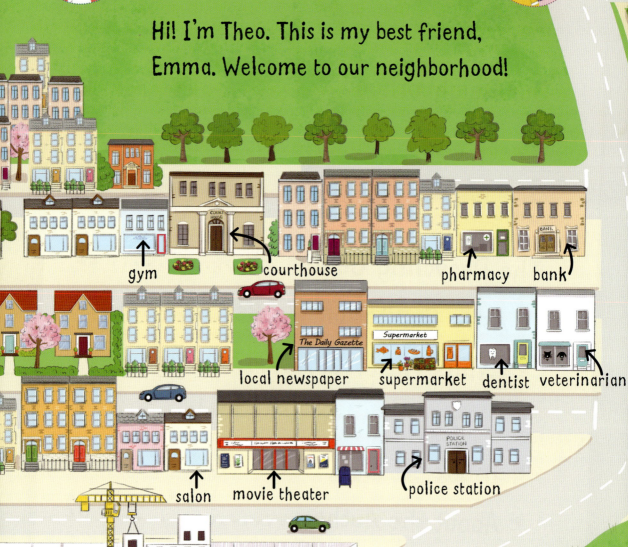

gym, courthouse, pharmacy, bank, local newspaper, supermarket, dentist, veterinarian, salon, movie theater, police station, construction site

Can you see the recycling center? It is over there. Emma and I got a tour last week. We had to do a report on community helpers for school. We chose sanitation workers. We wanted to know where our garbage goes!

We got the idea at lunch one day. Emma and I noticed how much trash we make in the cafeteria. We thought if everyone knew more about garbage, they would create less waste.

Can you see the recycling center? It is over there. Emma and I got a tour last week. We had to do a report on community helpers for school. We chose sanitation workers. We wanted to know where our garbage goes!

We got the idea at lunch one day. Emma and I noticed how much trash we make in the cafeteria. We thought if everyone knew more about garbage, they would create less waste.

MEET CELIA

Celia is a sanitation worker. She picks up our trash every Tuesday morning. Last week Emma met me outside my house so we could wait for Celia together.

Recyclables, such as plastic, metal, paper, cardboard, and glass waste, are placed in separate collection bins. They are picked up by a different crew.

When Celia pulled up, we told her all about our school project. She was happy to help!

"Trash collection keeps the neighborhood clean," Celia told us. "And making less trash helps keep the whole planet healthier!"

Food waste, such as fruit peels, food scraps, and eggshells, can be recycled, too. That is called composting. You can compost your waste at home!

Celia showed us the hopper. That's the part of the truck where the trash goes. She showed us what happens when the hopper gets full.

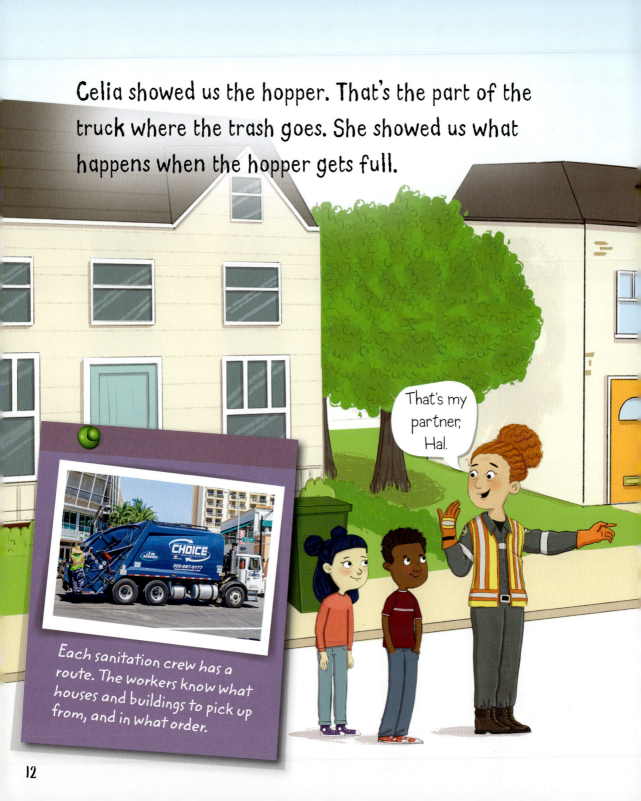

"That's my partner, Hal."

Each sanitation crew has a route. The workers know what houses and buildings to pick up from, and in what order.

CLEANING THE STREETS

"Picking up trash and recyclables isn't all we do," Celia said. "We also keep the streets safe in winter." When a storm is coming, the sanitation crew spreads rock salt. That helps keep ice from forming on the roads.

"A blade, called the compactor, smashes everything down. That makes more room," Celia explained.

CLEANING THE STREETS

"Picking up trash and recyclables isn't all we do," Celia said. "We also keep the streets safe in winter." When a storm is coming, the sanitation crew spreads rock salt. That helps keep ice from forming on the roads.

The team comes back after the storm to plow snow from the streets.

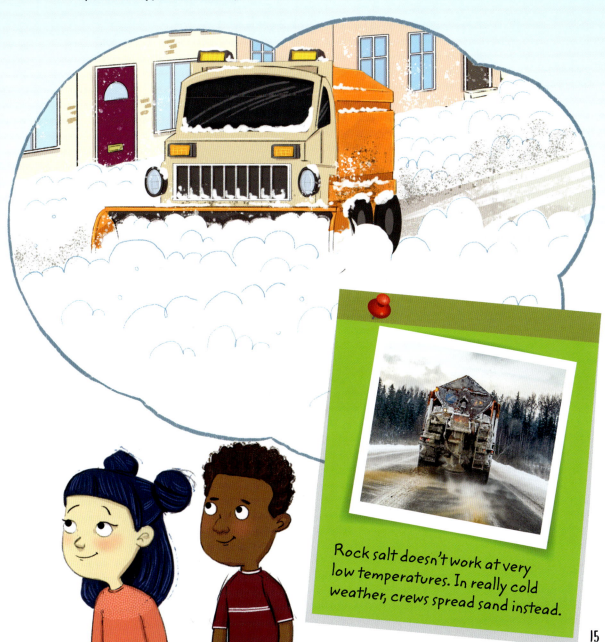

Rock salt doesn't work at very low temperatures. In really cold weather, crews spread sand instead.

15

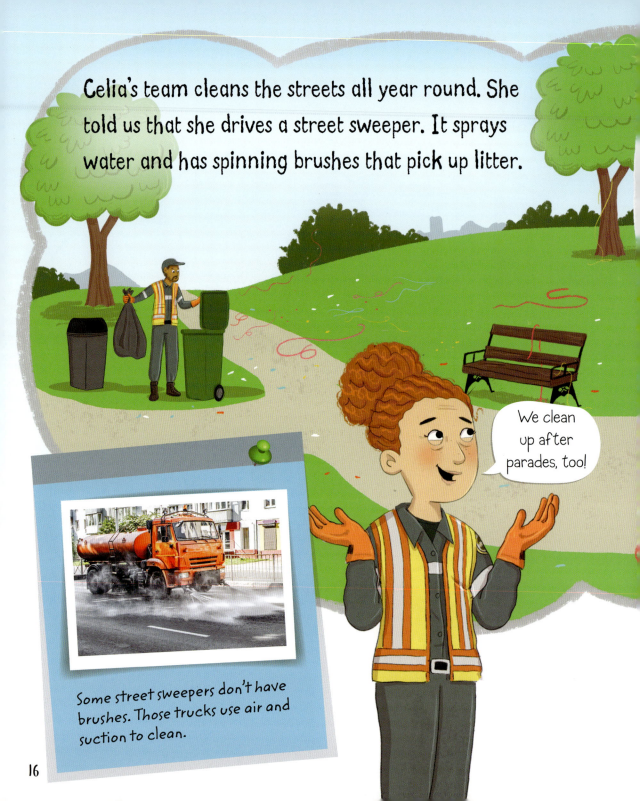

"We also empty public trash cans," Celia explained. "And we carry away leaves in fall."

"Where does the trash go after you collect it?" I asked.

Certain waste isn't picked up with the regular trash. It's too dangerous. This is called hazardous waste. Hazardous waste is handled separately and carefully.

"Our next stop is the transfer station," answered Celia. "There, waste is loaded into other trucks and taken to other locations."

I asked Celia what happens to garbage, recyclables, and hazardous waste after it is picked up from the transfer station. She explained the process to us.

Some trash goes to **landfills**, where it is buried underground. There are thousands of landfills in the United States.

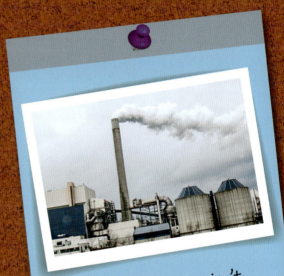

In some areas, there isn't enough room for a landfill. Instead, the trash goes to **incinerators** to be burned.

Then she invited us to visit the recycling center later in the week.

Some plastic, metal, paper, cardboard, and glass waste is sent to **recycling centers**. Then it can be prepared for reuse.

Certain products, including cleaners, paint, and batteries, are too dangerous to go to a landfill or an incinerator. Those are sent to **hazardous waste facilities**.

It would be better if we made less trash.

That's for sure!

THE RECYCLING CENTER

After school on Friday, my dad took Emma and me to the recycling center. Celia was waiting for us.

She told us that recyclables can be made into other products. "For example, plastic bottles and bags can be made into playground equipment," she said. "Recycled paper can be used for cereal boxes and toilet paper!"

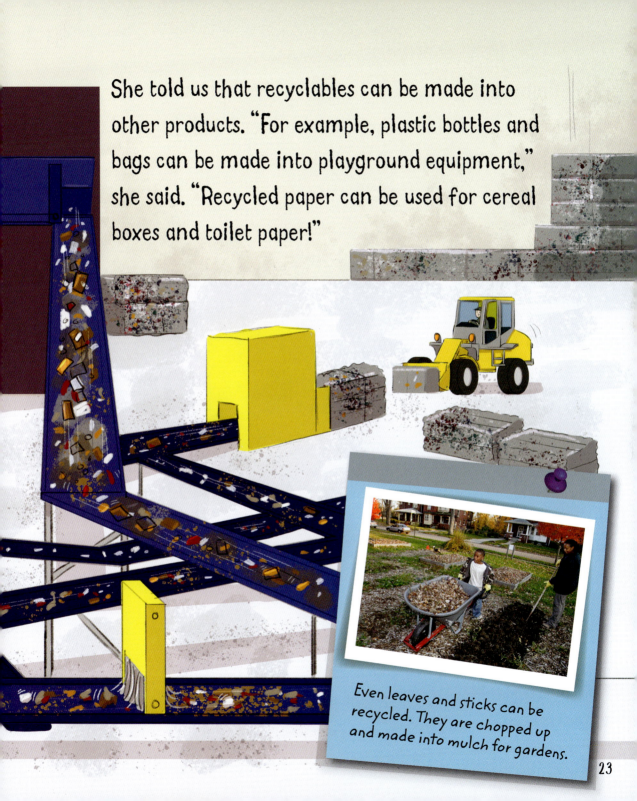

Even leaves and sticks can be recycled. They are chopped up and made into mulch for gardens.

Celia took us outside to where she'd parked her truck. She told us that keeping her truck in good shape is also part of her job.

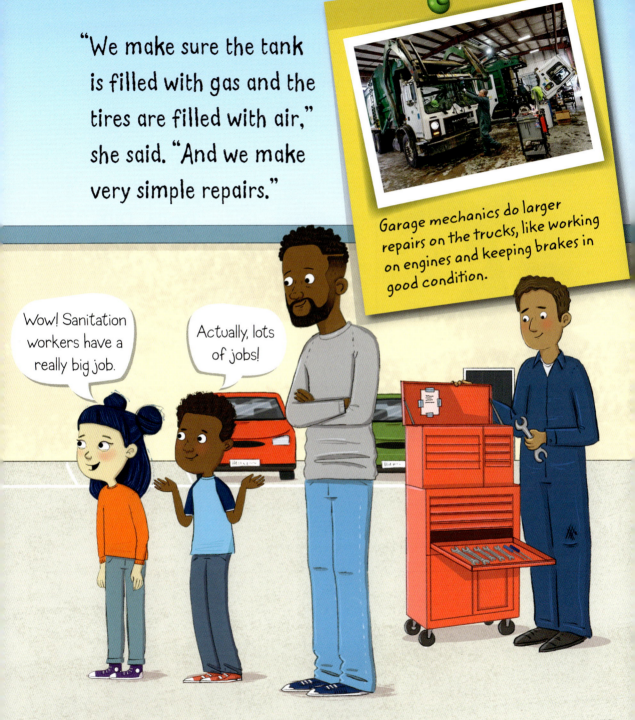

Emma and I gave our report to the class on Monday. It went really well!

"Celia and her friends work really hard," I said. "So let's do our part to keep our school and neighborhood clean."

Ask a Sanitation Worker

Emma asked Celia a few more questions about her job.

How did you become a sanitation worker?

Sanitation workers need to pass a written and a physical test. And we need to have a special kind of driver's license.

How strong does a sanitation worker have to be?

We have to be in good shape. Then we need to learn the safest way to bend and lift heavy loads so we don't get hurt.

What's the hardest part of your job?

I have to get up *really* early in the morning! Sometimes, like during snowstorms, I have to stay up really late, too.

What's the best part of your job?

I like working outside—though not so much on cold or rainy days. But the best thing is knowing I'm doing something important. I'm helping to keep the neighborhood safe and clean.

Do you mind the garbage smell?

I've gotten used to it! And I take a nice hot shower after my shift.

Celia's Tips to Help Make Garbage Collection Easier and Safer

- Slow down for garbage trucks! Sanitation workers have a dangerous job. They have to make many stops in traffic and walk around their trucks. Remind the adults around you to help keep sanitation workers safe.

- Be careful what you throw in the trash: Make sure sharp objects are not sticking through trash bags. Keep hazardous waste separate.

- Do what you can to make less trash. Take your own bags to the grocery store. Use a reusable water bottle instead of a throwaway plastic one. A plastic bottle can take more than 400 years to break down!

- Don't litter!